The OodleThunks

Oona Finds an Egg

THE OODLETHUNKS

OONA FINDS AN EGG

ADELE GRIFFIN
ART BY **MIKE WU**

SCHOLASTIC PRESS
NEW YORK

Library of Congress Cataloging-in-Publication Data available

ISBN 978-0-545-73279-6

10 9 8 7 6 5 4 3 2 1   16 17 18 19 20

Printed in the U.S.A.   23
First edition, January 2016

Book design by Phil Falco and Mike Wu

For Priscilla, my Oona.
A.G.

For Penelope, my Eggy.
M.W.

WEST WOGGLE

Horsetail

Teenyberries

Fruitafossors

Dairy

Brutes' Cave

Bristlecones

Oodlethunks' Cave

Valley Market

South Wilderness

Listening Hill

SOUTH GLOGGLE ↘

"I'm Oona!
My left ear has double-good hearing.
My club's name is Clonk-It.
I'm the fourth-tallest girl in my class."

Here's where I got bit by a craybird, but I didn't cry (much).

"Here's my little brother, Bonk Oodlethunk.

He smells like grass and mud.
He still has his baby teeth.
His club's name is Bonk-It.
He can't sleep without his Luvie."

"Meet my mom,
Allison Oodlethunk.

She is crazy for shoes. She is always on the go.
Her hair smells like meadow flowers."

"Meet my dad,
Dave Oodlethunk.
His feet just want to stay home.
He loves kittens, sunsets, and lullabies.
He enjoys trying new recipes."

THIS-A-WOGGLE?
THAT-A-WOGGLE?

I, Oona Oodlethunk, need a pet!

Reason number one: I am always getting lost. Like right now.

Yes, right now I am lost.

I looked up Mount Urp, but I didn't see school. I looked down Mount Urp, but I didn't see home.

If only I had a pet fruitafossor! A fruitafossor would know the way.

But here's the bad news: My little brother, Bonk, is allergic to fruitafossors.

"Bonk!" I called up the trees. "Come down! This game is over!"

No answer.

I dragged my Clonk-It behind me, and I kept my ears open for sounds of danger. There's lots of scary animals where I live: woolly mammoths, wild dogs, and big, hairy bison. I did not want to end up as somebody's dinner.

That's why Bonk and I were supposed to stick together.

"When Oona starts the fun, Bonkster gets it done!" he'd yelled to me after school. Then we'd chased each other around Mount Urp until Bonk climbed a tree and disappeared.

Where was he?

Reason number two I needed a pet? It could sniff out a little brother!

Ahead, I heard the sound of rushing water.

My left ear twitched.

I must be close to No-Name River.

But that wasn't Dragknuckle Bridge ahead. That was a skinny bridge.

A drop of water splashed my nose. I looked up at the sky. Uh-oh. Rain.

No Bonk. Wrong bridge. Now rain.

Bad day!

Whenever I am feeling my feelings, I yell. Sometimes my feelings are worried. Sometimes my feelings are scared. Sometimes my feelings are just plain mad.

But I always need to let them out.

I pictured my fruitafossor guiding my path over this strange, narrow bridge. Then I took a deep breath and let out my best

AAAAAAAAAAAAAA
AAAAAAAAAAAAAAH!

And I charged that bridge as fast as a mountain rabbit. I'd made it almost all the way across when—

SNAP!

BANG!

The bridge ropes were not holding! It was collapsing—and it was taking *me* down with it!

SWOOSH!

SWISH!

Bumpity-bump-bump I went, skidding sideways along the slippery, rocky riverbank.

Roly-poly bumpity-plop. I bounced to a stop.

Ook. That hurt.

Double ook—was that my shoe bobbing along in the water?

Durrr. It was.

Raindrops were smacking my face as I got my balance.

Reason number three I needed a pet? It could retrieve things! Like shoes!

How would I get my shoe back? I gripped a handful of picketwire that grew along the bank. Then I reached and stretched and poked my bare foot . . .

and . . .

and . . .

Got it! Good work, toes!

I hauled myself up and stuck my shoe back on. Whew! Plus I'd crossed the river into West Woggle.

Now I just needed to get home.

As I scooted to safety, my arm brushed something smooth.

I squinted. A wha—? A huh? Was it a tortoise shell?

No, this shell was smoother. And bigger. And kind of egg shaped.

I wiped rain from my eyes. "Hey, what are you, you great big egg-shaped thing?"

No answer.

"Huh!" I looked closer. "You aren't just a great big egg-shaped thing. You are a GREAT BIG EGG."

It was bigger than big. It was gigantic. The gigantic-est egg I'd ever seen. Also, it was beautiful. Its shell was the pale yellow of a new-morning sun. Its pattern reminded me of freckles on the tip of Mom's nose.

What was inside this giant egg?

A woggalizard? A craybird?

Was it dangerous?

Reason number four I needed a pet? To guard me against scary creatures that might hatch out of giant eggs!

Carefully, I placed my hand on the shell. Nothing happened.

But an egg meant a mother was near, right?

I checked over both my shoulders.

Nope. No mother.

I stood in the rain and slimy mud, planted my hands at my waist, and spoke low, the way Miss Gog taught us in our morning Grunts and Bellows class.

"HELLO?" I called. "HAS SOMEBODY

LOST AN EGG? BECAUSE I HAVE JUST FOUND A HEEEE-UUUUGE ONE!"

Nothing. Not a rustle. Not a growl.

I scooted down close to the egg. My heart was all thumpity.

"What are you, Egg?" I whispered.

Poor Egg. It didn't know that it had slid from its clutch, rolled down a mountain, lost its mother, and didn't have a chance of surviving this rainy night. Not unless I, Oona Oodlethunk, helped it.

I looked up and down Mount Urp.

I looked over the water where a bridge used to be.

Nobody was claiming this egg. It was an orphan. And you don't just leave an orphan cold and wet in the mud next to a broken bridge, do you?

No, you don't.

I put my mouth close to where Egg's ear might be. "Don't you worry, Egg," I whispered. "I've got a plan."

BURROW
DOWN

The rain had stopped and the moon was bright by the time I reached home. My legs were mud crusted, my stomach was empty, and my back—where I'd strapped Egg—felt like a boulder had dropped on it.

But I had not let go of Egg.

I set Egg gently in the grass by our cave, and I joined my family out back at the fire pit.

"Oona is late! Oona is late!" hollered Bonk. Then he picked up his dinner bowl and broke it over his head.

"Oona, where have you been?" Mom rushed to hug me. "We were so worried!"

"We were going to beat the West Woggle Neighborhood Drum and start a search party!" said Dad.

"Yeah, and I was gonna eat your dinner," added Bonk.

I gave Bonk a grumpy face. "I got lost on Mount Urp. Then I took a different bridge home, and it collapsed."

Mom handed me my bowl of vulture vittles. "That was probably Rattletrap Bridge. It's always collapsing."

"You've got to be careful, Oona. We live in dangerous times," said Dad. "Falling bridges, rock slides, and terrifying animals are just daily life in West Woggle."

"Double danger for Oona, since she gets lost so easy," said Bonk. Then he burped and blew it at us.

"Good burp," said Mom. "Smells healthy."

"Eat and pick your teeth quick, Oona," said Dad. "There's more rain to come. We'll want to burrow down tonight."

"Rainstorm! Rainstorm!" Bonk bared his teeth and banged his Bonk-It.

"Bonk!" warned Mom. "Save that face for predators."

"Storm, storm." Bonk grunted more quietly. "I know! I'll stuff the cave cracks with moss!" He jumped up and ran inside.

"Here, Oona. Let me get those bristlecones out of your hair," said Mom. "I'll use my T. rex–tooth comb. It can take out any tangle."

"Thanks, Mom." I gave a nice loud burp of my own. Then I leaned back. Bonk was such a baby. He didn't even have his grown-up, rock-grinding teeth. He could never talk around the table slab while licking dinner off his hands, like me.

"How was the rest of your day, Oon?" asked Mom. "Besides that bridge falling down, of course."

Should I tell my parents about Egg? I had to. It was too big to hide.

"I found an egg on the other side of Mount Urp," I said. "A giant orphan one! So I brought it home!"

"Big enough to eat?" asked Dad.

"Bigger," I admitted.

"Oona, that was risky," Dad warned. "Remember, in West Woggle, what you can't eat might eat you."

"Oh, Dave, it's probably a dud," said Mom. "Eggs don't last without their mothers."

"I want to take care of it," I told them. "What if it's not a dud? What if Something Cute is inside? Something Bonk is *not* allergic to?"

"Sure, Oona. You can take care of an *egg*," said Dad.

"Yes. Your *egg* has a home here for as long as it likes," said Mom. "If it hatches, then we'll decide what to do with the hatchling."

Hatchling! How Something Cute did *that* sound?

"Eeeeeeeeeeeeeeeeeeeeeeeeeeeeeeeeee!" I said, feeling my feelings.

Mom set down the comb. "All done. No more tangles."

"Did you ever see a real T. rex, Mom?" I asked.

"Great glaciers, no!" Mom laughed. "T. rexes haven't lived in West Woggle since Great-Grand-Oodles and Great-Grand-Thunks were alive."

"Fact: T. rexes were deadly meat eaters that walked on two legs. Fact: They had two clawed fingers on each hand." I loved dinosaur facts.

Dad shuddered. "Fact: The last Wogglian to see a T. rex was old Mr. Thagomizer, and you can't trust his eyesight."

Lightning zagged across the sky. "Time to move our fire indoors," said Mom. "This storm might be a doozy."

I carried Egg inside the cave, where it was cozy and warm. Bonk had tamped moss into all the cave crannies. While Dad and Mom built up the fire in the Great Room, Bonk and I changed into our extra-warm wolf-claw pajamas.

Then I checked on Egg.

"You can relax. You're home now," I told it. I patted down some extra moss and rolled Egg on top of it. Then I set out a bowl of water. Just in case.

When I climbed onto my upper bed ledge, I was sad that Egg was all the way across the cave.

Reason number five I needed a pet? Cuddling at night!

"Mom," I called out when she came over to give good-night nuzzles, "if my egg hatches, and the Something Cute inside makes Bonk sneeze, do I get to keep it anyway?"

"So far, that is just an egg," answered Mom. "An egg that Dad and I are letting you watch over."

"What do I get, if Oona gets a pet that makes me sneeze?" asked Bonk from his lower ledge.

"All you deserve is a clonk on the head," I growled. I was still annoyed with Bonk for abandoning me on Mount Urp.

"Trilobites could swing your Clonk-It better than you," said Bonk.

"Hush, kids," said Mom. "Let's let Egg sleep peacefully. Good night."

Once Mom and Dad had settled in the way back of the cave tunnel, Bonk's head poked up at the edge of my ledge. "Would you share your egg, Oona, if I help you take care of it?"

"No way." I frowned. "You left me alone in the wild, Bonky-Wonk. "

"If I hadn't left you alone, you wouldn't have gotten lost and found an egg. So that egg is here partly because of me, Oony-Moon."

Grrr. Bonk was a little bit right, but he was mostly wrong. "I hope whatever hatches out of my egg makes you sneeze your nose off," I told him.

Luvie and all her stains:

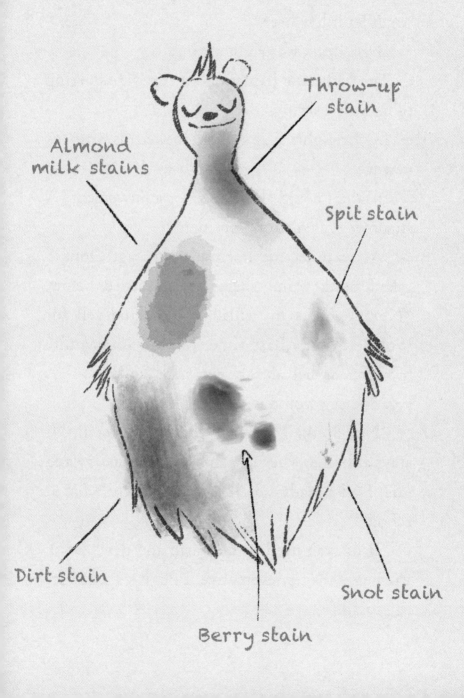

Throw-up stain

Almond milk stains

Spit stain

Dirt stain

Berry stain

Snot stain

"If it makes me *too* sneezy, Mom and Dad won't let it live here."

Grrr! Bonk was right again.

The flickering flames of our fire were starting to make me sleepy.

By firelight, Egg's shell looked as thin as new ice.

Inside, I could almost see . . . a movement? A shadow? A shadowy movement?

"At least let me borrow your egg, Oona?" asked Bonk from where he'd resettled below. "Next week is my turn at show-and-yell for Woggle Scouts. Last time, Meadow Stalagmite brought in her dumb pet rock collection. A gigantic egg would be way cooler!"

"No, Bonk. That's *my* egg," I answered. "It stays at home, where it can be warm and dry and safe. Dad already said he'd watch it while I'm at school."

"It doesn't need to be warm and dry." Bonk yawned. "It's not even alive. I bet it's a tortoise-egg fossil."

"It *is* alive, and you CAN'T borrow it, the end," I snapped.

"You *always* say no." Bonk banged his Bonk-It so the ledge shook. "I'm changing your name to Oo-no!"

"Stop banging your club, or I'm telling."

"Good night, Oo-no!" But he stopped banging.

"Good night!" I rolled over. But then I rolled back to look across the cave one last time.

"Egg is *not* a fossil," I said out loud. "It's going to hatch into Something Cute. I'm not telling a tall tale, either. I know what I know by *instinct*."

Bonk didn't answer. He was already asleep.

I was glad my little brother couldn't hear my thoughts. Because truthfully, I didn't know if that egg would hatch. Or what it might hatch into.

In fact, I didn't know anything about Egg at all. Egg was a mystery.

E-Z Recipe
for Vulture Vittles

yum

BRUCE ON
THE LOOSE

"Could Egg have been frozen on the top of Mount Urp?" I asked at breakfast the next morning. "It was cold when I touched it."

Dad scratched. "Maybe. Parts of Upper Urp never thaw out."

"So you think Egg could unfreeze to hatch into a live baby something?"

"Sure," said Dad, but it didn't seem like he cared. Not the way I did. "Now who wants a crepe?"

"What's a crepe?" asked Bonk.

"It's a thin pancake treat. In my recipe, I stuff them with mushrooms."

"Ew. I don't like mushrooms." I swallowed another handful of my breakfast teenyberries.

"I *hate* mushrooms," said Bonk.

"Even if you don't like mushrooms," said Dad, "I will always try to sneak them into your healthy meals."

"I don't 'don't like' mushrooms—I HATE mushrooms!" said Bonk, banging the table slab.

"And I don't like the *h* word," said Dad.

"Okay, Oodlethunks! My meeting is this morning. What do you think?" Mom raced up to present her tablet.

"'It's not just a wheel'?" I read. "Uh, Mom? That looks just like a wheel to me."

"Nobody knows what to do with a wheel. So we're advertising that it's not *just* a wheel." Mom had on her loud work voice. "We want everyone to know that wheels can do things!"

"Like what?" asked Bonk. We all stared at the "inspiration" wheel Mom had lugged home from the agency last week.

So far, it had just sat on our lawn.

"Good point." Mom drank her veggie smoothie. "Wish me luck."

"Good luck, honey," said Dad. "Give 'em your best Allison Oodlethunk. The one who clubbed my heart."

Mom beat her chest and burped. "I'll be home before the moon!" she said, and stomped off.

"Dad, you're watching Egg while I'm at school, remember?" I said.

"I remember. Here, kids. Don't forget lunch."

"Thanks." I took my school sack from Dad and peeked in. Ew! Fried newt fingers and dandelion crumble?! Dad's lunches were so embarrassing.

Bonk was staring sadly into his lunch sack, too. But he didn't complain. Dad was sensitive about his recipes. "Come on, Bonk," I said. "Let's go."

Before we left, I kneeled to nuzzle Egg. Suddenly I didn't want to leave. What if Egg got lonely? What if Dad forgot about warming it in the sun? What if Dad's bad singing voice got

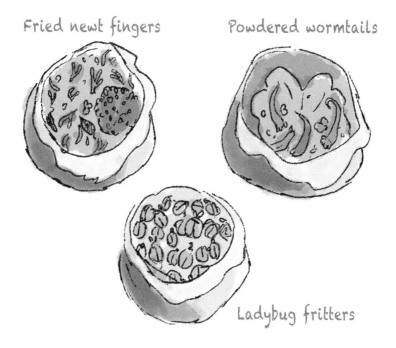

Fried newt fingers

Powdered wormtails

Ladybug fritters

Egg upset? "Be a good egg, Egg," I whispered, "I love you."

Egg didn't answer. I hoped it didn't miss its mother. I hoped it wasn't scared I was leaving it.

"I heard that!" Bonk snorted. "You just said 'I love you' to a rock!"

"It's not a rock, Bonk."

"I know my rocks. That's why I'm a one-pelt Woggle Scout." Bonk beat his chest. Then he sniffed. "Something stinky is outside."

"Are you sure?" I asked.

"Smells like old scrambled eggs," said Bonk. "Gotta be you-know-who."

Eeeeyich. I knew who that was. This morning, the wildflowers in the mountain breeze also held that rotten-eggs and badger-bottom smell of—

"Bruce Brute!" I pinched my nose.

Bruce Brute:
The Most Annoying Boy in West Woggle
- Does not like water, so he never takes a
  bath (pee-yoo!).

- Always asks too many snoopy questions.
- Lips, teeth, tongue are usually always stained with apricot juice.
- Ears are crusty with earwax.
- Always has some underpants showing since he pulls them up too high over his belly button.
- Never cuts his toenails until they start to grow under.

Bruce Brute lived across the path. His family owned the Brute Dairy. That meant Bonk and I were neighbors with the most annoying boy in West Woggle. But Bruce was not just annoying because of his Bruceness. He was annoying because of his tricks.

Super gross tricks.

Super gross tricks were what Bruce Brute did best.

Like he could pick his nose with his tongue. Super gross. Bruce could also roll his own earwax into a ball and shoot it out of his nose. Double super gross. And last year, on a dare, Bruce ate eleven live wriggling worms. Eleven!

(He didn't even get sick. He said worms tasted like scrambled eggs.)

Bruce was always trying to get my attention. This morning was no exception.

"Why are you waiting for us?" I asked him.

"Because I have a question for you, Oona," said Bruce. "Last night I saw you come home really late."

"You're such a cave creeper, Bruce!" I scolded.

Bruce acted like he didn't hear me. "You were carrying something heavy on your back. And you were being really careful. Was it a valley-melon?" Bruce licked his lips. Bruce loved food—mostly scrambled eggs. But he would eat anything. Also, he would eat everything.

"Nope. Sorry, Bruce." I shook my head. "It wasn't a valley-melon."

"Yeah, it's a secret!" shouted Bonk.

"Be quiet, Bonk!" I elbowed him. If Bruce thought there was a secret in our cave, he'd never stop till he found out what it was.

"I meant it's *not* a secret," said Bonk, winking at me. "Last night, Oona brought home a big bag of bison boogers!"

"I said be quiet, Bonk!" I warned.

"Bison boogers?" Bruce looked interested. Then he looked mad. "Nah. You're not telling the truth."

I nudged Bonk. "Let's go." We began to walk to school. Fast.

"Oodlethunks! Wait for me!" yelled Bruce.

We didn't speed up, but we didn't slow down, either.

Mom and Dad had a rule: Be kind and thoughtful. To everyone. Including Bruce Brute. Even if Bruce was not kind and thoughtful back. "Be kind and thoughtful" was rule number two on our cave wall.

"On the wall means it's the law," Mom and Dad liked to say.

1. No biting

2. Be kind and thoughtful

3. Don't club the furniture

4. Grandma Grandthunk
gets the best sleep pelt

5. Wipe your feet

WHAT NOT TO EAT
IN WOGGLE

snoozewarts

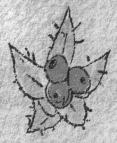

burpfruit

prickerwire

spidermold

WHAT ~~NOT~~ TO EAT
IN WOGGLE

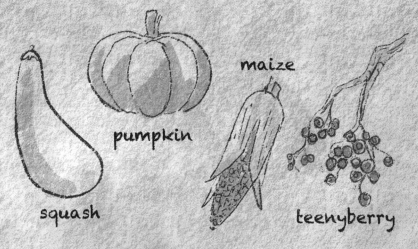

maize

pumpkin

squash

teenyberry

This morning, Bruce was not up to his annoying tricks. This morning, besides panting alongside us on the way to school, Bruce was snooping.

Snooping was what Bruce did second best.

Showing off was what he did third best.

Bruce didn't do anything fourth best.

But Bruce didn't know squat, I thought as I strode along. He'd been snooping around only the outside of the cave. Not the inside. He had no idea about Egg.

We all crossed Dragknuckle Bridge, clubbed through the brush, hiked up Mount Urp, then took Thorn Thicket Path all the way to school.

"Hey, Oona. If your dad uses that melon to make fruit salad, you'd better invite me over. Or else."

"Or else what?" I challenged.

"Or else I'll chop down your teenyberry tree." Bruce made a chopping motion with his hand.

"You're lying!" But inside, I felt sick. That tree was special. The berries that grew on it were too sour for most people, but not for me.

"Maybe I would. Maybe I wouldn't," said Bruce. He made the chopping motion again. My face burned red. But I didn't want Bruce to think he'd gotten to me.

I stormed ahead.

"What's around your wrist, Bruce?" asked Bonk.

I turned around.

"My bison-bone bracelet." Bruce gave his wrist a shake so we could get a better look. "My uncle Thuglass gave it to me."

"Can I borrow it?" asked Bonk. "I need something for show-and-yell next week."

"No way!" said Bruce. "Uncle Thuglass would be mad. This bracelet is from our Brutish ancestors. It was passed down from Mesozoic times."

"Bonk is too little to borrow things," I said.

"I am not too little!"

"Yes, you are. You'd probably break it or lose it," I said. "As your older sister, it's my job to remind you how careless you are."

"Bonk no break no thing!" yelled Bonk in cave-baby talk.

"That bracelet is too nice for you, Bruce," I said. "Your wrist is all grimy and dusty. You should wash in the river at least once a month, like the rest of us."

Bruce bared his teeth at me. "I'm scared of water, remember?"

"That makes you an even bigger baby than baby-talk Bonk," I said.

This made Bonk mad. He started waving his Bonk-It around and kicking up so much dust that I took off and ran the rest of the way to school.

If only I had a cute pet to come with me to school—instead of gross Bruce and babyish Bonk!

The morning horn hadn't sounded yet, so kids were outside, enjoying free play.

"Oooooona!" Erma Gurd, my best friend, waved and hopped just as I bounded over the hill. "Come quick! I've got news! It's big! It's life changing! And you're never going to guess it!"

Big? Life changing? Had Erma also found a giant egg?

I started to sprint.

NAME THAT
HABITAT

"Can you guess, can you guess, can you guess?" Erma grabbed my hands and spun us in a circle. Erma loved to spin in circles.

"Erma! Tell me, tell me, tell me, before I throw up from dizziness!"

"My best news is—I'm getting a fruitafossor! Iggy and I are picking him up at Primal Pets at the end of the week!" Iggy was Erma's little sister.

"Whoa," I said, dropping Erma's hands to stop the spin. We both staggered backward. "That is soooo lucky!"

"We are naming him Storm. Know why?"

"Why?" My heart tugged. Erma's news was way better than finding an egg. Erma was getting a real, live pet.

"Because Mom told us about him during that storm last night!"

"Storm is a perfect name!" I could feel the wistful stick in my throat. Lucky Erma! Lucky Iggy! Now the Gurd cave would have a sleep mat, a food bowl for Storm's termite dinners, a water bowl, a chewing bone—and a fluffy-faced fruitafossor named Storm to use all of those cute things.

Egg was also a pet. Sort of. Egg needed care and love. But Egg didn't do anything. Egg was only a responsibility.

Or at least, I felt a big responsibility for Egg. Even now, I was worried! Would Dad remember to set Egg on the long grass in the sun? Would he remember to switch her over to the shade?

What if Egg started to hatch while I was here at school?

Hoooooonnnnk! Miss Gog sounded the morning horn. We all lined up.

"Whatcha thinking, Oona?" asked Erma, flipping around to peer at me so close that both our sets of eyes crossed. "You've got your think-squint."

"Oh, nothing." I bonked my forehead against hers. Erma wouldn't want to hear about Egg—especially when she and Iggy were about to get a real pet.

"GOOD MORNING, KIDS!" yelled Miss Gog, who yelled everything.

"GOOD MORNING, MISS GOG!"

"ARE YOU READY?" she yelled.

"READY!" we yelled back.

"FEET ON MATS! GRUNTS AND BELLOWS STARTS NOW!" Miss Gog raised her arms high.

We scattered to our mats.

"STRETCHHHH YOUR ARMS!" yelled Miss Gog. "EVERY FINGER! OPPOSE THOSE THUMBS!" She gave a huge bellow. Some kids covered their ears. When Miss Gog got her bellow on, she sounded louder than a black-billed magpie.

I raised my arms high. I loved to stretch and grunt and touch my knuckles to my toes. Bellowing was harder. Unless it was in Tall Tales, I never let my deepest, strongest feelings out in front of everyone.

After Grunts and Bellows came Intimidation

Tactics with Master Og. I didn't like I.T., but at least Erma and I got to be partners.

We faced each other to practice our scariest faces.

"ARRRRR!" I bared my teeth.

"GRRRR!" Erma drew back her lips and snarled.

"You look like a fruit bat about to attack a pear for lunch!" I told her.

We both exploded laughing.

"Girls!" Master Og frowned. "If you're in hunting terrain, and you start to giggle when a camelop or a bison is on the prowl, you will be snapped into its jaws and chewed up faster than you can squeak, 'Oooh, please don't eat me!'"

"Sorry, Master Og."

"Now go forth and Intimidate!"

"Yes, Master Og."

We tried to keep our laughs in, but we messed up about six more times. Erma's face couldn't intimidate a mosquito!

After Intimidation Tactics came snack and rest, and then we all sat in the circle for Tall Tales. It was Bruce Brute's turn first. He told us about the time when he discovered a valley-melon that was as big as a boulder.

"I made a delicious melon fruit salad using ice from the top of Mount Urp. I shared it with everyone." Bruce looked at me and licked his lips. Yuck.

"That tale was *so* not tall," I said quietly. "It was not even medium." Some kids around me laughed. "Thanks for your tiny tale, Bruce," I said louder, for more laughs.

Bruce made a sneaky ax-chopping motion just for me. Grrr.

"OONA OODLETHUNK," said Miss Gog. "SINCE YOU ARE FEELING SO CRITICAL, WOULD YOU LIKE TO GO NEXT?"

"Yes!" I jumped up. I was great at Tall Tales. It was my best subject.

I stood in front of the class, and I struck a dramatic first pose: feet apart, arms wide. "Last night, I got lost on Mount Urp. It was raining hard, and I couldn't see my way home. As I crossed Rattletrap Bridge, it collapsed! 'Help!' I called. Nobody heard."

"Oooooooooooooooooooooh." Every face was watching me.

"It was bad enough to land in the wet, cold dark. But then I felt a heavy, scaly grip on the back of my neck."

"Ahhhhhhhhhhhh," said the class.

I took crouch pose. I made my hands like pincers. "It had deadly, clawlike fingers."

"Eeeeeeeeeeeeeeeeeeeeeee," said the class.

"I was too scared to run. When the clouds parted, I turned. That's when I saw the giant reptile's face. Its jagged teeth glistened by the light of the moon. There was only one thing this monster could be—a deadly T. rex!"

"Noooooooooooooooo!" roared the class.

"Yes! And it was in pain. As it lowered its head, I saw the problem. A bristlecone was stuck in its eye. It wanted me to use my fingers to pry

it out. I had no choice. I reached my hand up to its huge, gooey eyeball. Then, suddenly—*POP*!"

I pretended to prong a bristlecone between my fingers. "I was holding a bristlecone smeared in T. rex eye gunk!"

"Ewwwwwwwwwwwwwwww!" kids shrieked.

When I "threw" the bristlecone into the crowd, the class hollered and some heads even ducked.

"The grateful T. rex walked me safely home," I finished. "The end!"

Everyone bellowed and beat their clubs or their fists. I'd crushed it. I knew a five-pelt tale when I told one.

"CLASS? DID YOU BELIEVE OONA'S TALL TALE?" asked Miss Gog.

"YES!" they shouted.

"Not me," grumbled Bruce from the back. "Everyone knows T. rexes don't live in West Woggle anymore. Nobody's seen one in years."

"At least I know how to think tall," I said.

Bruce stuck out his tongue, but I didn't care. I always rocked Tall Tales.

After Tall Tales came lunch. Today we got to sit outside.

"Trade you my newt fingers for some saber puffs?" I asked Erma as we spread out our lunches on the grass.

"Uhhhhh." Erma peered over. "How about you keep your fingers, and I'll give you some puffs?"

"Thanks, Erms." Erma was such a good friend.

Sunshine was warm on my face. Was Dad watching? Egg needed sun, but probably not too much, or it would overheat.

"Your think-squint is back," said Erma.

"Urrrr, it's nothing." Maybe I *should* tell Erma about Egg. Except what if it *never* hatched?

"It's *something*." Erma shook her finger. "I know you, Oona. Also, you forgot to pick your teeth after snack, and you couldn't get into a comfortable position at rest."

I nodded. "Maybe I'll draw a picture of what's on my mind in art class."

"Funsie." Erma jumped up and brushed puff crumbs from her lap. "It's about time for art now. Let's sprint."

We dashed down the hill to the arts cave.

I loved the arts cave, where you could put anything you wanted on the walls. Today was freestyle paint. First I mixed my own shades of red and yellow and blue, using water plus brightly colored mineral rock powders. Then I daubed my paint-bone into my mustard-yellow mixture, and I began.

"What's that?" asked Erma after a while. Erma was painting Storm, of course.

"Egg," I said.

"What kind of an egg?" asked Erma.

"Not *an* egg. Egg," I said. "Egg. Egg is what's on my mind. I found it last night by No-Name River. I carried it all the way home even though it's as heavy as Bonk and it's as big as five Miss Moony heads." I had to whisper that part. Miss Moony was our art teacher, and her head was really big.

"Hey, is this a tall tale?" whispered Erma.

"No, it's true," I answered. "Egg is at home. It might hatch into Something Cute. But it doesn't have a mother. It might be a dud."

"Oona, what's this?" asked Miss Moony, as she stopped to inspect my painting.

"It's a painting of Oona's pet egg," said Erma.

"It looks lonely," Miss Moony decided. "What is its habitat?"

"Habi—what?" I asked.

"Habitat," said Miss Moony. "The living condition your egg needs to be happy. For example, an iguana egg lives in a different habitat than a raptor egg."

"Oh. Like its home," said Erma.

"I never thought about Egg's habitat," I admitted.

"Where did you find it?" asked Miss Moony.

"It came from the top of Mount Urp," I answered.

"Oooh. A raptor, most likely!" Miss Moony

gave a hop and a shiver. "Watch out, Oona! No matter how much care you give a raptor egg, it might hatch and eat you!"

Then she moved on to check out Thodunk Rode's painting of a volcano.

"A raptor!" Erma squeaked. "Oon, did you think of that? Your egg might hatch into Something Deadly!"

No, I had not! I was thinking about it now!

"Even if it *is* a raptor egg," I said, "Miss Moony is right. It needs a habitat. I should make a nest. I'll start by gathering puzzle grasses and palm fronds that grow by No-Name River."

"Yes! A nest!" Erma began to spin in a circle. "Super cute, Oon! I'll help."

"Great! It's more fun to build a habitat together."

"Ha-bi-TAT! Ha-bi-TAT!" Erma spun so hard she fell down. "After that, we can hunt for a chew bone for Storm."

My smile shrank.

But Erma was all excited, and I didn't want to hurt my friend's feelings. Erma deserved a pet fruitafossor! It wasn't her fault that she didn't have an allergic little brother!

"Great plan, Erma," I said, pulling her to a stand. "Let's do just exactly that."

HOW TO MAKE A NEST:
Start with the softest plants in Woggle

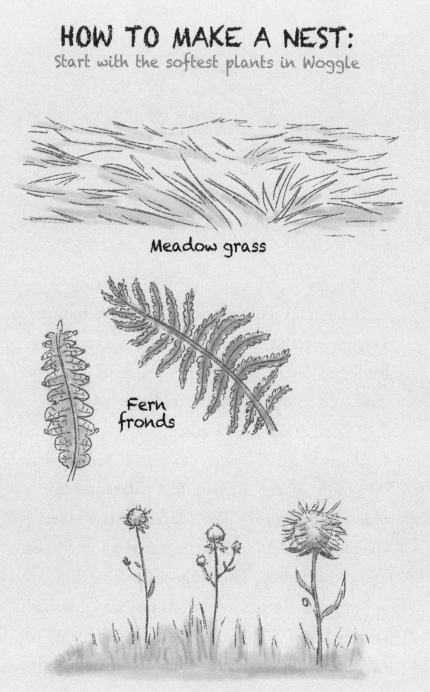

Meadow grass

Fern fronds

Sweet thistle

"BONK RULES WOGGLE!"

"I bet Eggy wants a pillow!" said Erma.

The school day was done. We were hunting treasures on the banks of No-Name River. We'd just found a stash of leaves, mosses, ferns, meadow grass, and soft plants to create Egg's habitat.

"What's a *pillow*?" I asked.

"A sack stuffed with feathers," said Erma. "My mom invented them. She's already made a bunch to bring to Valley Market this weekend. The only problem is that the feathers sometimes fall out of the top. Then it goes flat."

I nodded. "A pillow sounds perfect." I waded past my knees in the water. I'd collected plenty of leafy fronds, and now I was going after the lily pads.

"You should paint pictures of other eggs and flowers in Egg's cave corner, to brighten it up," Erma suggested.

"Great idea. I want to get some sweet thistle, too. What egg wouldn't enjoy the scent of sweet thistle? Do you think it can smell through its shell?"

"A deadly raptor has an excellent sense of smell!" Erma reminded me.

I tried not to think about Egg as a deadly raptor enjoying the scent of thistle before it ate me. "Come over for a playdate," I said. "I'm sure Dad made snacks."

When we got home, I saw that Dad had set out a plate of black-bean brownies. Urk. He'd also set Egg under the shady teenyberry tree.

"Eggy-Weggy-Woo!" cooed Erma, dropping to her hands and knees. "Look at you! You are the most cheerful shade of yellow I ever saw! And oooh, those shell speckles!"

I smiled proudly.

Mom was already home from work. "Hi,

girls! The clients loved our not-just-a-wheel campaign!" she called. "They even gave me a basket of apples. Dad's using them for his apple stew—and, Oona, you take the basket. Egg can nest in it."

"Thanks, Mom!" I picked up the large straw basket. "The handle is sturdy enough to carry Egg around."

"Let's stuff the leaves and fronds in there," said Erma.

We prepared the basket and settled Egg. As the sun set, we carried it inside.

"Eggy looks peaceful in her Egg nursery," I decided. "I think I'll paint her wall tonight."

"Now let's find Storm's bone, before it gets too dark," said Erma.

I nodded. A deal was a deal.

Outside again, we beat our clubs around in the nettles, searching for the best chew bone. But we couldn't find a single one.

"I bet there's more bones by the bristlecone trees," said Erma. "Come on."

We plunged into the heart of the woods. From high above in the hollow of a cypress, a pair of vultures watched us. I imagined Eggy hatched into a baby vulture and pecking at me with her huge beak.

"Ouch!" Hard shells rained down on my head.

Above me, I heard Bonk laughing.

"Cut it out, baby brother!" I shouted to the trees.

"When Oona starts the fun, Bonkster gets it done!" called Bonk.

"I didn't start anything!" I hollered.

"Hey, Bonk!" sang Erma. "Come down and

help us look for a chew bone for my new fruita-fossor! The right bone is so hard to find!"

"Hard? You mean easy!" Now Bonk appeared from his hiding spot to front-roll over a branch, drop, and land on his feet. He flared his nostrils at us. "I'm a one-pelt Woggle Scout. I can smell out a bone as good as any scavenger."

"Whatever," I said. "We've been looking for a really long—"

"Ooo—ooo-ooof! Rrrf! Wuff!" Bonk was on all fours. He dug around, sniffing. When he looked up, he had a bone in his mouth.

"Thanks, Bonk!" said Erma, taking the bone. "You remind me of a wolf! A wolf with perfect eyesight."

"Bonk rules Woggle!" Bonk wagged his bottom like he had a wolf tail. Then he sat up and howled.

"Stop showing off for Erma," I said.

Bonk's cheeks turned red. "Was not."

"Was, too."

"You think you know everything in the whole flat world, Oo-no?" Bonk smirked. "But you can't even tell an egg from a fossil!"

"It's *not* a fossil, and now she's in her perfect habitat," I said.

"What's a habitat?" asked Bonk.

"It's too hard to explain a big word to a little kid," I told him.

"I was kidding. I know what habitat means. I just forgot for a minute. Kind of like how *you* forgot that a fossil egg can't hatch, reptile brain!" Bonk's whole face was red as lava and his eyes were shiny.

"At least *I* don't need my special Luvie blanket to sleep!" I said.

Now Bonk's face went almost purple, and his tears were in danger of spilling out. But Bonk would never cry in front of Erma.

Instead, he turned and ran.

"Hey, Bonk! Thanks for the bone!" called Erma. "Also, a habitat is the home that Eggy needs to be happy!" She looked at me. "I don't think he heard."

"Oh, who gives a woggle about Bonk?" I said. "He can be really primordial."

"He did find us the perfect bone," said Erma, holding it up to inspect.

It *was* a nice bone. The exact right size for a baby fruitafossor.

I tried not to care, but my mind made a sad picture of Bonk's hot, embarrassed face. I shouldn't have teased him about his Luvie in front of Erma.

Even if my head felt dinged from where bristle-cones had smacked me. It couldn't hurt worse than my mean words.

And I was still the big sister.

I should have been kind and thoughtful.

I'd just have to figure out a way to make it up to Bonk. He looked pretty mad.

A STINKY
STORY

"Wakey-wakey," said Mom, tickling my foot. I cracked open an eye. No school today! I loooved sleeping late.

"What's that delish smell?"

"Berry almond mash. Bonk picked the fruits and nuts, and Dad made breakfast."

I was already up. A quick check on Egg and then—mmmmm! Mash!

"Thanks for the food-gathering, Bonk," I said as I pulled up to the slab. Bonk and I had not been too friendly last night. We'd stayed on opposite sides of the cave. I'd worked on Egg's habitat while Bonk had done pull-ups off the sleep ledge.

"No big deal." Bonk shrugged.

"Bonk," I said. "What are you wearing?"

"What, this?" He shook it. "Oh, this. Bruce is letting me borrow his bison bracelet for show-and-yell."

"Bruce did something *nice*?" Bruce was not that kind of kid. "What did you do for him?"

"Nothing," Bonk answered.

Nothing? No way. "There's something stinky about that story," I said.

"Maybe Bruce is turning over a new leaf," said Mom.

But I knew the only thing Bruce ever turned over was a new sneaky plan.

"Dad, can I go with you to Valley Market?" I asked, changing the subject. "I want to get Eggy a pillow."

"What's a pillow?" asked Mom.

"It's a soft sack, with feathers . . ." I couldn't remember if the feathers were on the inside or outside of the sack. "Erma's mom invented it."

"Yes, come join me, Oona," said Dad. "You can

look for pillows while I barter my Oodlethunk Delights. Bonk, are you in?"

"No. Bonk have googly-tummy," said Bonk.

"Don't talk in cave-baby, Bonk." Mom's eyes narrowed. "I do see some red splotches on your face."

"A couple of yellow ones, too," I noticed.

"Bonk! Did you eat any burpfruit when you were out gathering this morning?" asked Dad.

Bonk grunted. "I can't remember."

"But burpfruit is poisonous!" exclaimed Mom.

"Bonk, what do Mom and I *always* tell you about staying away from plants that give you the grunts?" asked Dad.

"You say, 'Try not to eat too many,'" said Bonk. "Looks like I ate too many." He grunted, burped, and sighed. "I'm sick."

"You stay home with me," said Mom, "while I re-bed the rock garden. It needs more rocks."

"That's settled," said Dad. "It's a father-daughter day. I will pack lunch."

"And you'll watch Eggy, Mom?"

"Yes. I'll give it sun, shade, and love," promised Mom.

"Thanks!"

Bonk didn't say good-bye as Dad and I left. He was curled up in a ball on his ledge. I wondered if he was still mad about how I'd teased him in front of Erma yesterday, or if he was really sick.

But I decided not to ask him.

It was a warm, sunny day to walk to Valley Market. On the way, Dad and I picked and sniffed and tasted roots, grains, berries, and blossoms.

"Food is everywhere," Dad said. "You've just got to know where to look. Observe, experiment, and record. See, you are stepping on cycads. If you boil the root of the cycad, you can make a tasty pudding."

"Fact: Stegosauruses liked cycads," I said. "They didn't make them into puddings. They ate them right from the ground—along with mosses and big rocks."

"Big rocks?" Dad made a face. "I like tiny, flavorful rocks."

"Big rocks helped stegs break down tough food. Stegs also might have thought big rocks *were* food. Miss Gog said nobody is sure. Stegosauruses had small brains."

"No wonder they died out," said Dad. "Big rocks taste terrible. Even when you add salt."

"What do you think Eggy will eat, once she hatches?" I asked. "I hope plants. I don't want to hunt down mice to feed to a hungry baby raptor."

"Just as long as Eggy does not eat you," said Dad. "Let's cross our fingers that Eggy's an herbivore."

I kept my fingers crossed all the way to Valley Market. It was busy. Everyone had something to trade. I helped Dad set up his Oodlethunk Delights stand.

"Dad's food has a cult following," Mom always told us.

That was her nice way of saying that not many people liked Dad's food.

But some people did. Soon we had traded a jug of apple stew for a gently used mortar and

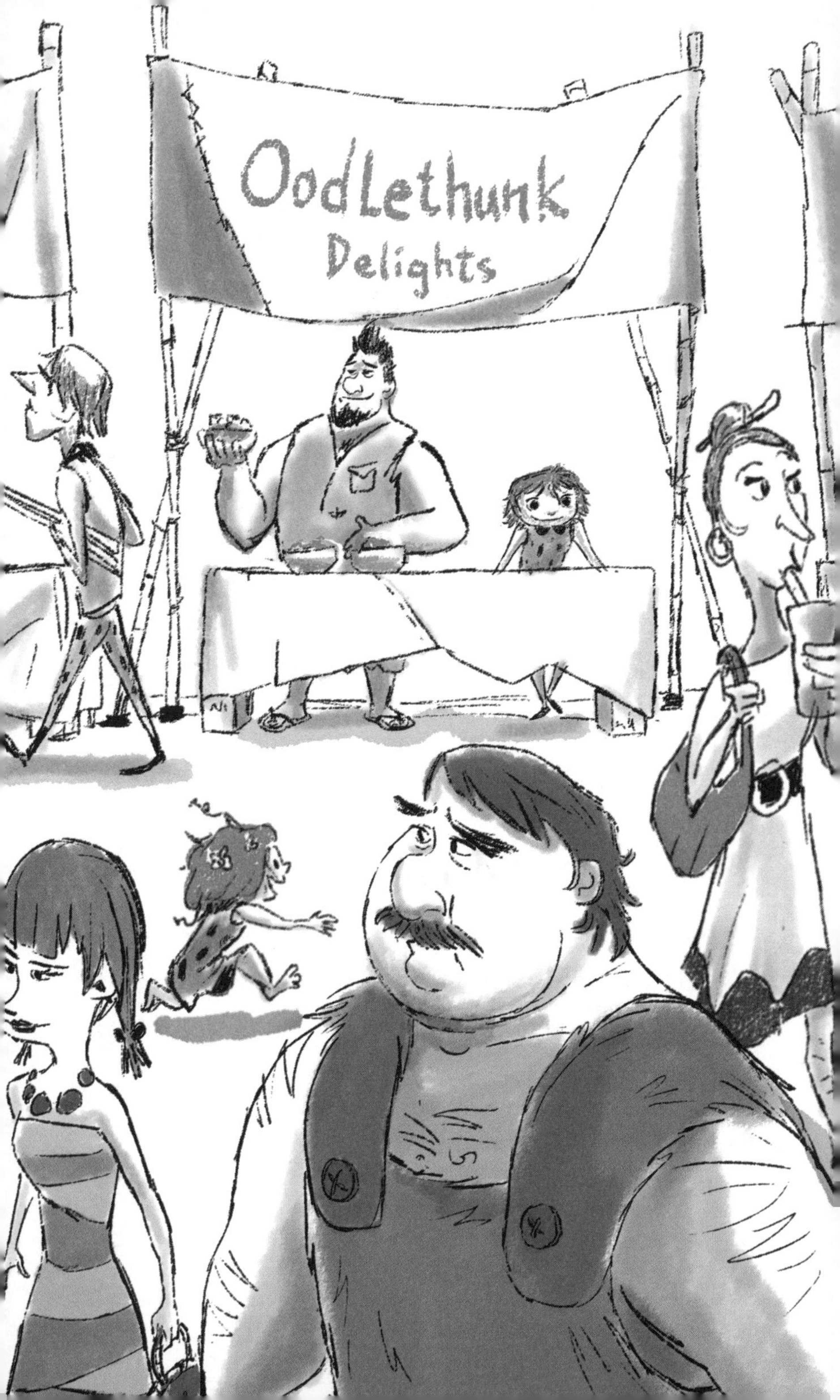
Oodlethunk
Delights

pestle. Dad also traded a sack of dandelion crumble for a pair of woolly slippers to give to Mom.

After that, business slowed down.

"Oodlethunk Delights aren't for everyone," said Dad. "I'm ahead of my time. Most folks want a chunk of meat, and that's it. The same old chew and swallow."

"Well, I'm a fan," I said, patting Dad's arm. "Hey, I want to see if Erma's mom's got pillows to trade. Erma said they might be bringing Storm, too."

"Let's meet here at sundown."

"You got it, Dad."

The market center was bustling. I traded a branch of teenyberries for a drink of apricot smash. Next I checked out the strong-man contest. Then I joined a large crowd on Listening Hill to hear Gerdy Droog.

Gerdy Droog was the best shot in West Woggle. She gave rabble-rousing speeches. I even had her *X* on my autograph tablet.

"Wogglians! We live in constant danger!" Gerdy's bellow carried all the way down the valley. "But whenever I'm on the hunting plains and I'm staring down a vicious tetrapod or hyaenodon, I remember one thing."

I'd heard this speech a lot of times. It was still really good. Most of the audience knew what was coming. We all shouted along:

"Fear! Is! Useless!"

And we whooped and swung our clubs and stamped our feet. Gerdy bared her teeth and showed a few intimidation tactics—all of them way better than anything my face could do.

Gerdy's speech was still ringing in my ears when I found the Gurds' Cozy Comforts stand. Erma was holding tiny Storm. She dropped him in my arms as soon as I rushed over.

Erma sighed. "Isn't he adorable? We're practicing attachment care. Which means we don't let baby Stormy out of our sight. Ever."

I buried my nose in Storm's wild fur. "Nice to meet you, Storm!" I scratched his ears. Storm's

tongue licked the tip of his button nose. He was
a pretty color, gold with white patches, and his
wet brown eyes sparkled like No-Name River.

Erma's mom reached inside her satchel. "I saved you a pillow, Oona. For your egg. Just hold it this way so the feathers don't fall out."

"Here, I can trade it!" I handed Storm back to Erma so that I could rummage for an Oodlethunk Delight—the last of the newt fingers.

"Oh, I couldn't, thank you. I just had a bowl of microgreens," said Erma's mom. "Besides, the pillow is a gift, not a trade."

"Thank *you*!" This pillow was so cute, stuffed to the top in feather softness.

"And Storm loves his new bone. Thank Bonk again, from me," said Erma.

"Will do." I felt a pang of Bonk-guilt as I hugged the pillow. Feathers drifted from the top. "Oooh, so soft. I can't wait to give this to Eggy."

"Even deadly raptors want to put their heads on soft pillows," said Erma, "as they dream of swooping down on defenseless prey."

I shivered at the thought.

Then I gave Storm one last scratch before saying good-bye to the lucky, lucky Gurds. When I found Dad again, he was sampling a chunk of Brute Dairy goat cheese.

Bruce's parents were both here, but thankfully—no Bruce.

"If I combined goat cheese with my home-grown lettuces and pomegranate seeds," said Dad, chewing, "I could make a delicious farm-to-slab salad."

"Mmm!" Bruce's mom patted her stomach. "Hi, Oona. I'm sorry Bruce isn't here. He usually loves coming to market. This morning, he wasn't feeling good."

"Oh, well." I tried to look sympathetic. "Next time." Was Bruce's mom aware that she had a kid as gross as Bruce? Come to think of it, a tiny Bruce would be the only thing worse than a baby raptor hatching out of Eggy!

I showed Dad the pillow as we began the walk home.

"So *that's* a pillow. Very nice." Dad test-hugged it. "Oona, you've made everything so

comfortable for Eggy that it might decide to stay an egg for good."

"That's okay," I said slowly. "Even if it's always an egg, it's still my pet." Privately, though, I didn't think it was okay at all. I really, really wanted Eggy to hatch. I knew I had to stop imagining a hatchling. But I couldn't.

Even if my hatchling had sharp claws and a hard beak, and might attack me, or fly away from me and forget all about me—even that was better than a dud egg.

I squeezed my pillow tight for the whole trudge back.

In the yard, Mom was right where we'd left her, digging up the rock garden. Bonk was sleeping on the wheel. "His spots have faded, and he ate quite a lot of stew for lunch," said Mom. "Poor little porcupine."

Bonk was snoring and drooling. He didn't remind me of a poor porcupine. He looked like a healthy kid brother with smudges on his face.

"Eggy!" I called, as I ducked inside. "Look what I have for you! A darling pillow!"

I saw Eggy's basket, lined with lily pads, meadow grasses, and fern fronds.

I saw the brightly colored eggs that I had painted on the cave walls so that Eggy could feel relaxed.

I saw the clay bowl of water that I always set out.

But I did not see Eggy.

Eggy was gone.

VANISHED

"Can we stop looking now?" asked Bonk.

"No!" I yelled. "It couldn't have rolled far! We have to find it!"

"Oona," said Mom, "please don't yell at your brother. It's not his fault your egg is missing."

"We've checked everywhere." Dad used both hands to scratch the top of his head. "It's a mystery. The only thing I can think that might have happened is—ah, never mind."

"What, Dad?"

"No. I can't. It's too terrible to say out loud."

"Say it!" I gulped.

"Okay. The only thing that might have happened . . . is that Eggy got taken."

"NOOOOOOO!" My knees went wobbly.

"But I don't understand . . ." Mom looked upset. "Eggy was in my sight nearly all day. There was only one true moment of danger."

"Tell me, Mom! I need to know."

"Eggy was under the teenyberry tree," Mom began, "looking very content. As the sun got lower, a shadow fell over me. I looked up and, well, Oona, I did see a red-tailed hawk. But I shooed it, and it flew off."

"Aha. A hungry hawk could have circled back and snapped up Eggy in its talons just like that." Dad made talons with his fingers.

No! Nothing was worse than picturing a hawk swooping down, its talons grabbing up my Eggy. This was one time I did *not* enjoy having an excellent imagination!

"I picked up the basket and moved it inside," said Mom, "and I went back to digging in the garden. Then you and Dad came home. It was only when I heard you scream that I realized something bad had happened."

"The hawk must have dived into the cave," said Dad sadly.

"Yeah, probably," said Bonk. "Anyway. I'm finished looking."

No way was *I* finished looking. There wasn't a habitat in West Woggle better than the one I'd created for Eggy.

Wherever Eggy was, she didn't belong there. She belonged with me.

I searched our cave inside and out. I turned over every rock and branch.

But I couldn't change the truth. Eggy had vanished off the edge of the world.

At dinner, I could only poke my fingers at my fiddlehead ferns. After dinner, I sneaked out of the cave and prowled around the yard, calling for my missing egg.

What in the woggle had happened to Eggy?

What creature would have been cruel enough to take her from me?

The next morning, I was up with the sun to look all over again. I hated that Eggy had spent the night away from me. Even when the others went outside to have juice and hemp muffins, I stayed in, looking, looking, looking . . .

I will never give up looking for you, Eggy!

Finally, I had to. I threw myself down on the cave floor. I remembered the first time I'd seen my orphan egg on the riverbank. I could feel again the ache in my shoulders and the lightness in my heart, carrying Eggy home that rainy night. How carefully I'd stepped, even if it had taken me triple the time.

I thought about all of Erma's and my fun, creating Eggy's habitat.

And I imagined my future self, tucking Eggy—hatched into a surprisingly gentle raptor—inside her basket for a nap.

The future was the cruelest part: The future that would *never come true.*

I lifted my head. "This is the worst day ever!" I hollered. "My first day without my egg!"

My voice bounced into echoes around the cave.

"I would give away everything! Everything I owned, including my Clonk-It and my paint set! I'd give away my own name, if it meant I could get Eggy back!"

Inside the cave was as quiet as falling snow. Outside, I could hear my family talking and ignoring me.

"You could call me Rmmph!" I shouted. "Rmmph Oodlethunk! If it meant Eggy came home!"

Nobody answered.

I dropped my head and closed my eyes. I let the sadness wash over me.

Eggy never even got a chance to have a nap on her new pillow. She was out there all alone, rolling around on hard surfaces, with nobody there to shout "Cliff!" or "Mountain lion!"

Nope, she was just rolling, rolling, rolling into danger . . .

I opened my eyes and saw my family's feet all around me.

"Oona. You can't lie on the ground forever," said Mom.

I was pretty sure I could.

"Sweetie, have a muffin," said Dad.

"No." I had no appetite.

Bonk nudged my side with his club. "Bonk-Bonk," he said. "Bonk-Bonk. C'mon, Oona. Say

'Who's there?' My Bonk-Bonk jokes rule West Woggle."

"Go away," I told him.

"Don't know why you're so crabby about a fossil," said Bonk.

"It wasn't a fossil," I said. "It was a responsibility. And I let it down. Now I will always wonder what happened to my egg. My heart is broken."

"I know, sweetie. But you still have to go to school," said Mom, "and you look sort of feral. Please let me run that T. rex tooth through your hair."

"Uhhhh," I grunted. What was the point of tidy hair, if Eggy was gone?

As if things couldn't get any worse, Bruce was waiting outside our cave.

"What's wrong with you, Oona?" He leered at me. "Did you eat so many teenyberries that your face turned sour?"

"My egg has disappeared," I said. "And now I'll never know what it was going to hatch into."

"Aw, that thing's just a dried-up raptor egg," said Bruce. "It probably belongs in a cool fossil collection."

"You never met Eggy, so how do you know?" I snapped.

"Yeah, Bruce!" said Bonk. "You never even saw it up close! Remember?"

"I know," said Bruce. "That's right. Sorry, Oona."

There was something twitchy and uncertain about Bruce's expression. As in, if Bruce were a small wild creature, and I had on my best intimidation-tactics face, then small-wild-creature-Bruce would run off squeaking.

"Come on, Bonk." I elbowed him. "Let's walk fast. I'm not in the mood for any more talking with Bruce Brute."

"Uh, me either," Bonk agreed. This time, we raced and left Bruce in our dust.

At school, Erma knew that something had upset me. "Oh, Oona!" she cried when I told her the bad news. "I bet your dad was right! It was that hawk! Or maybe a prairie dog took it? Or a great horned owl?"

"There's too many tragic endings to think about," I said. "I tried to take perfect care of Eggy. But in the end, I didn't do a good enough job."

"That's not true, Oona."

Except I knew it was.

After school, Erma gave me a good-bye hug. "Here," she said, reaching into her school sack and pulling out a walnut.

I stared. Two round eyes and a cherry-red mouth smiled up at me.

"It's a toy Storm, made out of a walnut," explained Erma. "I painted him at the end of Art. You can put it in your basket." She handed it to me. "I know Walnut Storm is not as good as Eggy. But it's not as bad as an empty basket, either."

"Thanks for thinking of me, Erma," I said. "Walnut Storm is really cute."

That night, lying on my ledge, with Bonk snoring below, I faced down the possibility that I would never see Eggy again.

Not only that, I would never know what happened to it.

I had never felt so sad in all my life.

"Good night, Eggy," I whispered. "Wherever you are. I hope if you are safe, that you hatch into a beautiful life."

My eyeballs ached from looking. My legs ached from running and seeking. My heart ached from missing.

I was one big ache. And all I had to show for it was my empty tomorrow.

Even though I couldn't see Walnut Storm in Egg's basket, I knew Erma was right. An empty basket would have been worse.

I could feel sleep coming on . . .

What was that? My eyes snapped open.

It sounded like a whimper. And a rustle. With a dash of mutter.

The fire had gone out. The cave was the heavy dark of just before morning.

Quick as a woggalizard, I skimmed down from my ledge to where Bonk shifted and muttered on the ledge below, with Luvie dropped over his face.

"Wake up, Bonk!" I shook his shoulder. "You're having a bad dream!"

Bonk lurched up. His eyes were wild. What

was wrong with him? Closer, I saw that his sick spots had smudged across his face. I couldn't tell if that meant he was sicker or better.

"Bonk! Are you feeling okay?"

"Rrrrhh," mumbled Bonk, rolling over. "Just a bad dream. Nothing a one-pelt Woggle Scout can't handle."

"Do you want to tell your dream to me?"

"Na," said Bonk.

"But Dad and Mom say you always should get your dream out in the open."

"Fine. I dreamed I found your egg." Bonk pulled Luvie back over his face. "Now let me sleep."

Suddenly I didn't feel tired. What if Bonk was right? What if Eggy was findable? What if Bonk had extra-good dream sense that could lead us to her?

Or! Or! Did my little brother know something that he was not telling me?

"Bonk!" I hissed. "Why are you *still* wearing Bruce's bison-bone bracelet?"

"He gave it to me. Here, you can have it." Bonk pulled it off and threw it at me. "I don't even like it anymore."

I slipped it on. It looked pretty good. "What do you want to trade it for?"

"Nothing," said Bonk.

"Nothing?" I repeated. "You're better at bartering than that, Bonk!"

"I don't care." Bonk yawned and flipped over. "Just take it."

Maybe it was because the cold air had woken up my brain. Or maybe it was the moonlight shining on the truth: that the smudge from Bonk's cheeks had also smudged onto Luvie.

My heart leaped.

"I can find Eggy, all right!" I said, jumping up and baring my teeth at Bonk. "Because you know where Eggy is! You *did* trade Eggy, didn't you, Bonk? You traded Eggy for Bruce's bison bracelet!"

"Did not," mumbled Bonk.

"Did so!" I acted it out like a tall tale so that Bonk could see it clearly. "You even blobbed spots on your face so you could pretend to be sick and stay home. *Then* you waited for the perfect opportunity! When I was at Valley Market with Dad, and Mom was busy in the garden, you sneaked Eggy over to Bruce's. *That's* why Bruce pretended to be sick, too! So he could be home for the handoff!"

"Urrrr . . . no?" Bonk spoke quietly.

"Urrrr, yes! I know I'm right!" I stamped my feet and growled.

"Don't scare me!" whined Bonk. "Anyhow, you weren't such a good big sister yourself, Oo-no! You shoulda let me borrow that egg for show-and-yell."

I stayed fierce. "Listen up, little brother!" I said. "You got me and Eggy into this Brutish mess. Now you need to make it right. Got it?"

"Got it." Bonk was twisting Luvie in his fingers. "But how?"

"By getting Eggy back. This minute."

"Eggy is safe with Bruce. He wouldn't hurt it. We'll go get it tomorrow."

"What? Imagine if I'd said such a thing, when that wild grabble had snatched you!"

Bonk didn't really remember when the grabble had snatched him. It was Dad's favorite story, and he got me to act it out whenever guests came over. I'd been the one who saw baby Bonk get snatched while he nap-nestled in a rock bed. I'd hollered my head off and scared the grabble, which then dropped Bonk on his head. Bonk got a lump on his head the size of a fist.

That had been one of my best bellow days. And Bonk was never truly right in the head after that. (I always liked to add that joke.)

"Oona, I'm scared to go outside. It's dark. There's predators."

"If it's dark for you, just think how scared Eggy feels! You owe me, Bonk."

"You owe me something, too," said Bonk. "Because you embarrassed me in front of Erma."

I knew what I owed Bonk. So I made those words come out. "I'm sorry."

"Apology accepted. But, Oona, if you had said you were sorry when I was doing my pull-ups the other night, I wouldn't have planned my revenge."

"I guess I was too excited about getting Eggy's habitat ready. You know that feeling, don't you, Bonk?"

My little brother nodded. "Yeah."

"Bonk," I told him. "Now there's really no more time to waste. Let's go."

Bonk jumped off his slab. He grabbed his club.

"Oona starts the fun," he said, "and Bonkster gets it done!"

It didn't seem like the right moment to tell Bonk that *nothing* about taking Eggy back from Bruce would be fun.

Would we get it done, though?

That was the question!

BY THE LIGHT
OF THE MOON

Smutch, Urg, Urch, and Murgatroyed were four girdle-lizards that had guarded the Brute Dairy since I was the size of a bump on a log.

The lizards were also stone-deaf. They kept snoring even after Bonk and I climbed over the Brutes' wall and landed—*Plonk! Plonk!*—on the ground in front of them.

"Ha, ha, ha, ha!" I laughed at each of them when we landed. "Four cabbages could guard the Brute Dairy better than you sleepy scaleys!"

We were standing in the Brutes' huge field. Was anyone watching us? I looked around and

tried out an intimidation stance. One hand on my hip, one gripped around my Clonk-It, and my feet planted wide.

"Bruce Brute, say hello to your worst cave-mares!"

"I'm nervous. Bruce will be mad at me," whispered Bonk. "He told me *never* to tell you about our trade."

"Don't even *talk* about that awful trade, you—"

"Shh!" Bonk put his finger to his lips. "What's that noise?"

Noise? My left ear twitched. The hair on the back of my neck stood up. "What? I don't hear a thing."

"I think it's coming from over there. By the goat pasture."

"All I hear is a low wind through the bristlecone trees. What does it sound like?"

"Like someone whispering," whispered Bonk. "Someone besides us, I mean."

"Lead the way, Bonk," I said. "Let's see your one-pelt Woggle Scout skills."

Bonk went into crouch pose. I followed.

We crept past the Brute family cave. We crawled up the path that led into the Brutes' upper pasture.

Where the moon was shining low and bright on . . . *Bruce?*

What was Bruce doing in the middle of the field? And what was he muttering about? As Bonk and I drew closer, one thing came clear.

"Bruce!" I snorted. "You still wear Snap E. Turtle pajamas? Ha, ha, ha! Those are soooo cave-babyish!"

Bruce spun around, clutching his hands to his heart. "Oona! Bonk! What are you two

doing here? Why are you spying on *me*—for a change?"

"Why are *you* whispering to yourself at night in your own goat pasture?"

"I don't think he's whispering to himself," said Bonk. "I think he's guarding something."

Guarding something? I lunged forward.

Was it? Could it be?

It was! It really was! "Oh, Eggy!" I felt dizzy with relief. Like Erma had just spun me in fifty nonstop circles.

My one and only Eggy!

"Eggy," I said softly. "I missed you so much! You look more beautiful than ever!"

In fact, Eggy looked so moon-glowingly, buttery-shell beautiful that, as much as I wanted to race over and throw my arms around her, I was almost scared to come closer.

"Its name isn't Eggy. Its name is Speckles," said Bruce. "And it *was* the best specimen in my already excellent fossil collection."

"Fossil collection!" I fumed. "That's no fossil."

"You might be right," Bruce admitted. "It can rock."

"It can *what*?" I squeaked.

Bruce cleared his throat. "It was rocking a little bit, inside the cave. And I didn't know what to do. So I brought it out here, just in case it—"

"Hatched!" I finished. I ran around Bruce to get a better look.

The egg *was* moving. Back and forth, back and forth, in a trembling dance.

And that's when I saw it. A fingernail-thin, jagged, splintering crack running along its front.

"Eggy. Is. Hatching." In front of my own eyes. I had hoped. I had wished. But I had never been one hundred percent sure this moment would happen.

My skin turned cold and prickly. My knees were so weak that I kneeled in the thistles.

"Wow. Get a woggleful of that!" Bonk had crept up on my shoulder. "You were right, Oona."

"Don't be scared, Speckles," said Bruce. "Hatch, Speckles! You can do it!"

"Come out, come out, not-a-rock!" said Bonk.

I kept quiet. I was the opposite of sound. I was only breath, in and out, hoping that Eggy could really do this.

Bruce and Bonk got quiet, too.

Chip-chip-chip . . .

"If it's a raptor, it'll be hungry first thing," I whispered. "And you're the biggest one of us, Bruce. Don't say I didn't warn you."

Bruce stepped back. "Do I really look that delicious?"

"Not at all," I told him. "But raptors aren't picky."

"What if it's a giant python snake?" asked Bonk. "Come to think of it, that looks an awful lot like a python shell. Once it's out, we're gonna have to jump out of its way quick."

A huge snake! I hadn't thought of that. "Don't worry. Bruce is the biggest, but he's also the slowest," I reassured Bonk. "A python would definitely swallow him first."

Bruce took another couple of steps back.

"Oona," said Bonk. "You know I'd never have traded Bruce his bison bracelet for an *alive* thing."

"I know. And I should have let you bring Eggy for your show-and-yell," I answered. "You *are* pretty careful."

"Also I don't think you're a reptile brain," whispered Bonk.

"And you're not a baby—" My words were interrupted by another *chip-chip-chip* from the inside of the shell.

"It's cracking! The egg is cracking!" said Bruce. He was standing pretty far away from it, so I didn't know how he could tell.

"Yes! It's breaking through!" said Bonk.

"There's the nose!" I pointed.

"You're right, Oona! You're totally right!" Bonk hopped around. "That is a nose!"

A nose that did not belong to a raptor. Or a python. Or a horned owlet.

Come to think of it, I'd only ever seen a wide, blunt, reptile-style nose like this nose at school, when the class had studied—

—DINOSAURS?

I could not blink. I watched the creature's nostrils flare and sniff as it kept prodding and poking its way out of the egg.

"Oona. What *is* that thing?" asked Bonk.

"I'm not sure."

"Please d-d-d-don't let it eat me," said Bruce.

"No promises, Bruce," I told him.

The shell continued to crack, crackle, and split. As the hatchling's nose punched its way through, the top of the egg dropped off, and we got our first good look.

We stared at the hatchling.

The hatchling stared back.

"I'm seeing it! But I just can't believe what I'm seeing!" I said.

"Me too," said Bonk.

"Me three," said Bruce.

The hatchling blinked and kept staring at us staring at it.

And then, with a high-pitched and ear-splintering "EEEEEEEEEE!" the creature stepped its two stumpy front legs out of the egg. It used its thick hind feet plus its long, double-plated-armored tail to shake off the rest of the shell, sending it sailing across the Brutes' grazing field.

The baby stegosaurus had arrived.

MINE!

"Baby Steg," I said. "You are one thousand times more adorable than a baby fruitafossor."

Baby Steg's head was small compared with her long, low, plated body. Her eyes were hooded, widely spaced, and green. Her mouth opened to reveal a long pink tongue and a double row of needle-fine, triangular teeth.

I felt like my heart was going to explode from her cuteness. I sat back on my heels. I squeezed my hands together. "Oh, what a beautiful morning!"

"This is crazy! Stegs are extinct around here!" yelped Bruce. "Aren't they?"

"Dinosaurs haven't been seen on Mount Urp since olden days," said Bonk.

"We're seeing one now. Guess this dinosaur is from new-en days," I said. "And she's mine."

"Correction. She's *mine*," said Bruce. "Cave law, remember. Speckles was born on my property."

My skin prickled. "Only because you stole her," I said.

"I didn't steal her. I traded her for my bracelet. The same one you're wearing!" Bruce pointed.

"Bonk just gave me this bracelet! I've barely owned it! Here—I don't want it! Not one bit! You can have it back!" I yanked it off and threw it at Bruce, accidentally hitting him on the ankle.

"Owie-owie-owie! That hurt!" Bruce hopped up and down. "Oona, you did that on purpose!" He slipped on his bracelet. "I'll keep it, and I'm keeping Speckles, too!"

"You can't do that, Bruce. All bets are off! I thought I was trading an egg fossil!" said Bonk. "Not a whole entire stegosaurus!"

I raised my Clonk-It and gave Bruce my best squint-eyed Gerdy Droog. "You don't want to get between me and *my* steg," I growled.

Bruce squared his feet and raised his club. "What makes you so sure?" he growled back, lower and deeper.

"Kids?! What's happening here?" We all turned to see Mom and Dad plus Mr. and Mrs. Brute standing behind the rock wall.

"You'll catch your death of cold out here!" Mrs. Brute shook her finger. "Bruce, where are your bunny slippers?"

Uh-oh. Grown-ups. A lot of 'em. Grown-ups always wanted to settle stuff differently. I lowered my Clonk-It. The sun was coming up, the rooster had started to crow, and all four sets of parent eyes were watching Bruce, Bonk, and me.

"Oona," said Dad, "you're the oldest. You owe us an explanation."

"Egg is a steg," I said, moving to the side and pointing to my baby steg.

All the grown-ups now saw Steggy. They gasped.

"Holy macaroni!" said Dad.

"Honey, what does that mean?" asked Mom.

"I don't know," admitted Dad. "It seemed like a cooler thing to say than *ugh*."

"Speckles hatched on Brute territory. It's *my* steg," said Bruce.

"*My* steg!"

"Says who?"

"ME, that's who! I found Eggy frozen on the riverbank! I brought her home and I cared for her with all my heart! She is my responsibility! And my pet!" I raised my Clonk-It.

Bruce scrambled for his club, too.

"Fight, fight!" hollered Bonk.

"Kids, kids," said Bruce's dad. "We can't solve this like savages. Well, maybe we can. But this stegosaurus belongs to nobody except the wilds where she came from."

"Steg doesn't even have a mother or a father," I cried. "She's an unfrozen orphan."

"That's true," agreed Mrs. Brute. "And a baby. A large baby. But still, much too small to be all on her own."

"So who gets to keep her?" asked Bruce.

"At my job, we go with who's got the most persuasive campaign," said Mom.

"That's it!" exclaimed Mr. Brute.

"What's it?" asked everyone else.

"Oona and Bruce will each call to the

stegosaurus," explained Mr. Brute. "The steg will choose who gets to care for her."

"Too easy!" Bruce sneered. "Speckles has been living with me for almost two whole days. She knows my voice best."

"All she knows is your smelly breath that she probably couldn't wait to get away from," I said. But my stomach kinked with worry as I stared at Steg, who was testing her wobbly legs and nibbling at a rock. Losing Steg to Bruce Brute was the most unhappy thing I might have ever imagined. It was the most awful tall tale I ever could have told—and worst of all, it might be true!

"Getting each kid to call out to the steg sounds reasonable to me," said Mom.

"Agreed," said Mrs. Brute.

"Bruce and Oona. Each of you turn and walk ten paces from the baby steg," said Dad. "Count it off."

Urg. After all my care of Eggy, and it came down to this? A count-off plus a callout? What if

Steg had a bad sense of direction, like me? What if she wanted to come to me but walked the opposite way?

This was terrible! Too much could go wrong!

Bruce bounced his ten paces to one end of the field. Of course he made sure he'd picked the downhill end, an easier walk for a new-walking steg.

I was so upset I could hardly remember how to count to ten. I shook my head to clear it.

Then I walked ten paces in the opposite direction.

Oooh! I was soooo far away from Steg! Now I'd have to rely on exactly what I didn't have: a big, strong bellow.

"Here, Steg!" Bruce yelled. "Here, Speckles! Come on, there's a steg!"

Some loose teenyberries were rolling around in my pocket. I chewed and swallowed them to push past the lump of fear in my throat. "Here, Eggy!" I called nicely.

"Come on, Speckles!" commanded Bruce. "Time to join the Brute family!"

Steg took a step toward Bruce. I licked my finger and held it up to feel which direction the breeze blew. Then I stepped into the best angle for the wind to carry my voice.

I needed all the help I could get.

"Come on, Steg," I called, trying to match Bruce's loudness but keeping my voice kind. "I know a lot about dinosaurs. I will take excellent care of you!"

Bonk, who was sitting on the top of the wall between Mom and Dad, now beat his chest with his fists. "Louder, Oona!" he called. "Shout like I hear you when I'm pelting you with bristlecones!"

Louder, louder, right. Got it. "Here, girl!" I yelled in a medium bellow.

"Come on, Speckles!" No fair! Bruce had a naturally louder voice than I did.

"I have a basket for you to sleep in!" My heart

was still pounding. How could I hold up my head in Woggle if my steg rejected me? "And soft leaves and mosses. Oh, Steg! Remember this lullaby I used to sing to you? 'Hush little Eggy / don't say a word. / Maybe you'll hatch into / a non-predator bird!' And you did!"

As I sang, Steg cocked her head. Her heavy-lidded eyes seemed to be listening to me.

But when I was finished singing, she took another step toward Bruce. And then another, and another.

Noooooooooooo! The worst was happening, step by step! Steg was now halfway to Bruce.

Tears stung my eyes.

"Yeah, girl, that's it! I'll feed you worms!" called Bruce at the top of his voice. "Lots and lots of wiggly worms! And all the scrambled eggs you want! Just think, worms and scrambled eggs all day long!"

"ARE YOU CRAZY? STEGS DON'T EAT SCRAMBLED EGGS AND WORMS!" I bellowed. "STEGS ARE HERBIVORES! THEY EAT FERNS AND LEAVES! DIDN'T YOU EVER PAY ATTENTION IN RECENT-HISTORY CLASS?!"

My whole body was twitching with outrage! Of course Steg should live with me! Bruce Brute's cave was not an option! What was I so scared of? As Gerdy Droog always said: Fear! Is! Useless!

"COME BACK, STEG!" I bellowed my bellowiest. "COME BACK TO YOUR REAL HOME!"

My voice echoed all the way down the valley.

Something was happening.

For the first time since the count-off, Steg stopped moving. She turned. She looked over her shoulder.

Her gaze was long and level on me.

Her expression seemed to catch a distant memory.

Her nostrils flared.

"Also, I love you." I didn't even say that part loud. But I said it from the deepest feelings in my heart.

With a tremendous "EEEEEEEE-YYUUURRRK!" followed by a long noisy snort and a flip of her plated tail, my Eggy-turned-Steggy marched on her big flat feet right back to her start point.

And then she walked:

  one

    two

      three

        four

          five

            six

              seven

                eight

                nine

                  ten more stumpy paces

into my waiting arms.

She nuzzled my face. I scratched her ears. And I knew that my very own Eggy, who had hatched into this perfect stegosaurus, was mine again. My heart melted with joy.

"I, Oona Oodlethunk, am the luckiest girl in West Woggle," I said. "You aren't what I thought you would be, Steggy. But you are so much better. And I am going to take such good care of you."

Steggy's eyes seemed to know exactly what I meant.

"Eeeeeeee-yuurrrrk," she agreed.

COMING NEXT . . .

**ANOTHER WEST WOGGLE
ADVENTURE, STARRING OONA.**

**AND INTRODUCING HER BRAND-NEW
CUTIE—STACY STEG OODLETHUNK!**

PLAYDATE!

Can I tell you something? My pet egg hatched into a baby stegosaurus.

I named her Stacy Steg Oodlethunk.

Stacy is the cutest steg I ever saw. She understands every word I say. She *urmp urmp*s when she is happy. She sleeps on the edge of my bed slab and warms my toes at night. Sometimes my toes feel smushed the next day, but how many kids get to keep a steg on the bed?

Stacy is hard work, but I don't mind. I'm always learning new things about her. She likes mosses and berries for breakfast. She enjoys walking through Woggle Woods. She cuts her tiny teeth on rocks. And she always stomps over to No-Name River to check out her back plates in its reflection. She is proud of her plates.

"Stacy is one active little steg," said Mom one night at dinner.

"She is also one hungry little steg," said Dad. "Today, while the kids were at school, Stacy got into my zucchini patch. She ate everything."

"Good job, Stacy!" Bonk banged his Bonk-It. "Zucchinis taste like snot, only without the good boogery flavor!" He leaned down and scratched Stacy behind her ear.

"Wrong answer, Bonk," said Dad. "We need those zucchinis for winter."

"Sorry, Dad," I said. "I'll find more breakfast for Stacy tomorrow, so she won't get the munchies."

But the next day, Stacy ate all of Dad's kitchen seasonings.

"My cinnamon, paprika, and mint—all gone!" he said. "I think we should tie her up."

"Nooooo, Stacy won't like that!" I cried. "She needs to roam!"

"Stacy is only part pet," said Dad. "She is also part wild."

"Urrr! I'm part wild, too!" Bonk jumped on the dinner slab and began to dance.

"Bonk, get your stinky feet out of the bone broth," said Mom. "And yuck, I need to cut your toenails. They're curling under like a craybird."

"We'll keep Stacy on a long lead so she can roam," Dad assured me.

But the next day, Stacy was in trouble again. This time with Mom.

"Stace ate my best straw-braided sandals," Mom said. "That steg does not have good instincts. And she is getting too big."

"Too big for what?" I asked.

"Too big for here," said Mom. "Stacy is outgrowing us. Her tail alone is as large as a lying-down Oodlethunk. She needs to fend for herself."

"But she can't survive out there!"

"She'll be fine out there," said Dad. "Stacy has no natural predators."

What crazy Oodletalk! I put my hands over my ears and waggled my head.

The next day was no school.

"And you know what that means, Stace," I said. "PLAYDATE!" Stacy and I didn't know any other dinos, but she was buddies with my best friend Erma Gurd's fruitafossor, Storm. We tried to get them together whenever we could.

Another thing I'd learned about my steg— she got along with everyone!

I was glad to take Stacy out of the cave for the day. Before we left, I gathered a triple helping of mosses and berries for her breakfast. I also made her a special trail mix: thistles, pebbles, and sunflower seeds. Stace was so happy to see all of that food that she slurped my face completely wet.

"Pelt up today, Oon," said Dad. "Gonna be a cold one, and the Gurds live pretty high on Mount Urp."

I pulled a pelt over Stacy, too. It only covered her to the middle.

By the time we got to Erma's cave, Stacy had finished her trail mix.

Erma's mom was sitting outside next to a huge mound of moss. "Hi, Oona. Look what I invented." Erma's mom was always inventing new, cute things. "I call these earmuffs," she said. "Here's a pair for you." Then she stuffed each of my ears full of moss. "To keep out the cold, see? You can have that pair."

"Thanks," I said, though they felt kind of scratchy.

I led Stacy into the Gurd cave to Erma's room, where Erma showed me Storm's latest trick.

"He can stand and balance a termite on the tip of his nose!"

She tossed him a termite. Storm jumped onto his back legs and caught it neatly on his nose. Then he ate it.

"That's so sweet!" I said. "Stacy doesn't have pet tricks yet. Her main trick is eating."

"Let's teach her how to sit," suggested Erma.

"Okay." I looked Stacy in the eye. She seemed ready for anything.

"Sit!" I told her.

Stacy leaned over and carefully used her mouth to pluck one of my earmuffs out of my ears.

"She's smarter when she's not hungry," I said. "Stace, don't eat my other—"

Before I could finish my sentence, Stacy had snarfed my other earmuff.

"I guess that was her trick," I said.

"She's smart in her own way," agreed Erma. "And she's growing so fast."

"You don't have to remind me. Last night, Mom and Dad told me they want to turn her loose! But where would she go? What would she do?"

We looked over at Stacy, who was now showing Storm how to chew the feathers out of Erma's pillow.

Erma squeezed my hand. "Have no fear, Oon. We're in this together, and we'll make a plan for

Stacy." I knew Erma meant it. She'd helped me care for Stacy ever since she was an orphan egg that I'd found on a rainy night.

"Time's running out," I told her. "Stacy's bigger every day."

We watched as Storm climbed up on Stacy's head for a nap. "I wish you had a magic recipe for Stace to be small forever." Erma sighed.

Magic? Magic! My idea split straight through me like *boom*! Like how Dad chopped a valley-melon in summertime. "I've got it!"

"What?"

"I think I've figured out how we can keep Stacy in our cave!"

"Tell me!"

"I'll do better," I said. "I'll show you. Tomorrow, after school!"

"Cool!" said Erma. "It's on."

AUTHOR'S NOTE

There is a lot of fiction in this story. But some facts are mixed in there, too. You might not recognize it, but the Oodlethunks' cozy West Woggle has many similarities to Denver, Colorado, in a post-Cretaceous Age. Many of the mosses, fronds, ferns, fruits, nuts, and conifer trees, as well as general topography, are true to that region.

Fruitafossors were real, North American, termite-eating mammals whose fossils have been uncovered in the Colorado area, along with the fossils of mastodons, woolly mammoths, various sauropods in the brontosaurus family, and variations of the deadly torvosaurus.

The most complete skeleton of a stegosaurus was also discovered in Colorado. In fact, it is the official state fossil of Colorado—and is the inspiration for the Oodlethunks' very own Steggy!

ABOUT THE AUTHOR

Adele Griffin is the highly acclaimed author of numerous books for middle grade and young adult readers, including the popular Witch Twins and Vampire Island series. Her novels *Sons of Liberty* and *Where I Want to Be* are both National Book Award finalists. Her latest novel, *The Unfinished Life of Addison Stone*, was a *School Library Journal* Best Book, a *Booklist* Top Ten Arts Book for Youth, an Amazon YA Book of the Year, and a YALSA 2015 Best Fiction for Young Adults Selection. She lives in Brooklyn, New York, with her husband and two children.

ABOUT THE ARTIST

Mike Wu is the author/illustrator of the critically acclaimed picture book *Ellie*. He is a top animator, working first for Walt Disney and then Pixar, where he animated such Oscar winners as *The Incredibles* and *Toy Story 3* among others, including *Brave*, *Ratatouille*, and *Up*. He is also the cofounder of Tiny Teru, a baby-and-toddler boutique featuring all hand-drawn items. Mike lives in Northern California with his family.